Five Days to Go!

WENDY GRAHAM

Illustrated by Naomi C. Lewis

Contents

CHAPTER ONE

The Problem with Mitchell

Jonathan stepped onto a low stool to reach the calendar. He marked a big **X** over today's date. Then he counted how many days were left. Five.

Five more days until his big brother Mitchell would go away to overnight camp. Jonathan could hardly wait!

It wasn't that he didn't like Mitchell—he did! He was just always there. In the way. Spoiling things. Like yesterday on the last day of school.

"Let's have a race," Mitchell called. "First one to the gate wins!"

Off he ran, leaving Jonathan to follow. Mitchell was *always* first.

When they played with their plastic building bricks, Mitchell always built bigger and better things than Jonathan. Mitchell built spaceships. And a tall crane with hook and chain. He knew how to winch it up with the little handle, too.

Jonathan wanted to learn how to do those things. By himself. Without Mitchell.

CHAPTER TWO

Building Sand Castles

It was Saturday and there was no more school. Jonathan marked another day off the calendar. Four days until Mitchell would go away to overnight camp.

"How about a day at the beach?" Mom and Dad asked them.

"Great!" they shouted, and both ran to get their things.

Jonathan stepped into the shallow waves. The cold water swished around his ankles.

Mitchell waded into the bigger waves, right up to his waist! "Come on in, Jonathan," he called. "This is great!"

"I don't need to," answered Jonathan. "It's great here, too," he said, splashing his feet.

After a while, Jonathan collected sticks, shells, and seaweed to make a sand castle. He worked hard and built a large castle.

It was lined with shells, and there were doors, windows, and a tiny flag made out of seaweed on the top. Then Jonathan made pathways all around.

Mitchell made a sand castle, too. He built a fortress—a huge fortress!

It was also lined with shells, and there were doors, windows, and a tiny flag on the top, as well as pathways all around. There were turrets, a drawbridge, and a moat with seawater in it.

"Look at mine!" Mitchell said.

The boys were tired that night. At bedtime, Mitchell climbed the ladder to his top bunk and Jonathan hopped into his own bunk below.

Jonathan wished he had the top bunk. But of course, Mitchell got the top bunk because he was older.

Once the lights were off, Mitchell always said to Jonathan,

"Night-night,
sleep tight,
don't let the naughty bed bugs
bite."

And Jonathan always answered, "You, too, Mitch."

CHAPTER THREE

"You'll Catch Up One Day"

The next day was Sunday, and Jonathan marked another day on the calendar. Three more days until Mitchell would go away to overnight camp.

In the afternoon, Mom and Dad took them to the skating rink. Jonathan was slow putting on his helmet, knee pads, and ankle pads. And it was hard to balance on the skates.

Mitchell was already racing around the rink. He took long strides in time to the music.

Jonathan stepped onto the rink, holding onto the rail. The skates were very wobbly! He took a few steps and grabbed the rail again. His brother flew by, waving.

When they arrived home, Mom began to make a cake. Mitchell got to hold the beaters, while Jonathan held the bowl.

Later, when the cake was cut, Mitchell got the very slice that Jonathan wanted, the one that had three strawberries on top instead of two.

"You can watch TV for a little while now," Mom said.

The brothers settled down to watch. Jonathan sat in the armchair because Mitchell always got the big sofa. Mitchell stretched out his legs and put a pillow behind his head.

Jonathan wished he could have the big sofa to watch television.

"You'll catch up one day," Dad always said. "After all, Mitchell is older than you."

But Jonathan knew he would *never* catch up. Because Mitch would *always* be older than him.

He couldn't wait for Mitchell to go to overnight camp. Next morning, he marked another day off the calendar. Two days left!

CHAPTER FOUR

Good-bye, Mitchell!

"Come on, Jonathan," Mitchell said. "Let's play a game of basketball."

Jonathan almost got the ball through the hoop. He tried a

number of times and was sure he could get it through if Mitchell wasn't there.

Instead, while Mitchell kept making baskets, Jonathan spent most of his time chasing the ball along the ground and across the lawn.

"Butterfingers!" called Mitchell.

Only one day left!

The boys played on the swings in their yard. Up into the air Jonathan swung, as high as he could go. "I can see over the fence!" he shouted.

But Mitchell swung higher and higher! "I can see over the trees!" he shouted. "I can see the town!"

Up he'd go again. "I can see the world!"

No matter how hard he tried, Jonathan couldn't swing that high.

In the morning, Jonathan climbed onto the stool and marked the last day off the calendar. Tomorrow, Mitchell would go to overnight camp.

All day long, he looked at the clock every few minutes. It was the slowest day he'd ever known.

He hurried through his dinner and went to bed early.

When Jonathan woke up, he jumped out of bed. It was the day he'd been waiting for. Mitchell was leaving for overnight camp.

Jonathan helped Mitch pack. "Don't forget your toothbrush," he said, smiling.

"Thanks, Jonathan."

"And your pajamas."

"Thanks, Jonathan."

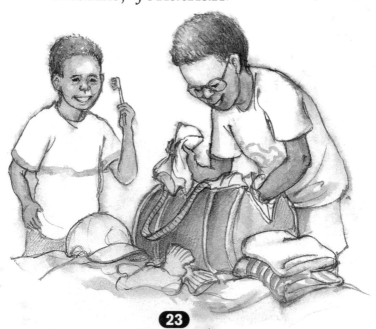

"Here, Jonathan," Mitchell said, "you can play with this while I'm away." He gave Jonathan the special racing car that he'd gotten for his birthday.

"Oh, thanks, Mitch!" Jonathan said.

Although Mitchell often let him use the car, Jonathan could not wait to zoom it along the floor, all by himself. Without Mitchell.

Mom, Dad, and Jonathan went to see Mitchell off to camp. They all laughed as Mitchell made funny faces through the camp bus window.

When the bus left the parking lot, Jonathan felt a funny feeling in his stomach. But he couldn't wait to start doing things, without Mitchell.

CHAPTER FIVE

Without Mitchell

At his own day camp, Jonathan joined some friends from his group to eat his lunch. Then he hit a ball against the wall for a while. It felt strange not having his brother around. But he was sure he'd get used to it.

After camp, he played with Mitchell's racing car. He spread out the traffic mat, and placed the car at the Stop sign. He revved up the wheels. Then *Zoom!* it took off, fast as could be, across the mat, and all the way to the wall.

But there was nobody to push the car back to him.

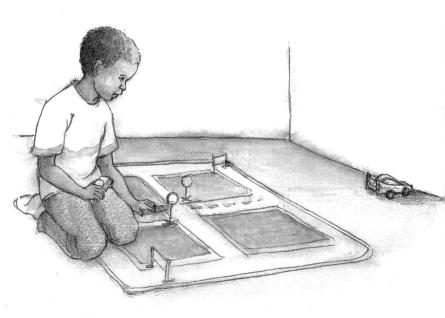

He took out the plastic building bricks. Now he had all the bricks to himself—every one! He started to build a garage.

In a little while he stopped. Maybe he'd finish it tomorrow. He didn't feel like it now.

Outside, Jonathan climbed onto the swing and up he went. Up and down, back and forth. Mitchell's swing stayed still beside him.

Sometimes Mitchell would twist Jonathan's swing around and around for him, so that when he let go, Jonathan would spin.

Today there was nobody to twist the swing for him.

Jonathan took his bicycle from the shed and began to ride it around the backyard. He and Mitchell always had the best fun racing around on their bikes.

Jonathan rode as fast as he could to the fence and back.

After he did it a couple more times, he wheeled his bike back into the shed.

Inside the house, he turned on the TV. At last, he could lie on the big sofa to watch TV, just like Mitchell always did.

Jonathan wiggled and twisted around. "This is a lumpy old sofa," he thought. He went and sat in his own chair. The TV show began, the one he always watched with Mitchell. It was funny, but somehow, he didn't feel like laughing.

At the dinner table, Jonathan sat alone with Mom and Dad.

It seemed very quiet without Mitchell, who was always talking.

"Well," said Mom, "how was your day, Jonathan, now that Mitchell is away at camp?"

Jonathan frowned a little. "It was okay," he said.

Dad smiled. "Somebody might think you miss him," he said.

CHAPTER SIX

Five Days to Go!

When it was time for bed, Jonathan brushed his teeth and thought of Mitchell. When Mitchell brushed his teeth, he would make a moustache with toothpaste and then wet his hair to make it stand up, all spiky. Jonathan would laugh.

Jonathan finished brushing his teeth and went to his room.

He looked up at the top bunk. Now was his chance! He climbed the ladder and laid down on Mitchell's top bunk.

It seemed very high up.

There was only a narrow rail. He looked over the edge.

What if he went to sleep and rolled over and fell all the way to the floor?

In a little while, he climbed down the ladder again, and hopped into his own bed. He closed his eyes.

"*Night-night,*
sleep tight,
don't let the naughty bed bugs bite," he said to himself.

Then he switched off his bed-
side lamp.

The next morning, Jonathan got up and pulled the stool to the calendar. He put a big **X** on today's date, and he counted how many days were left. Five!

Five more days until Mitchell came home. He could hardly wait!